This book is to be returned on or ...

For Elinor and Barry
V M

For Alice
and with thanks to George,
Tom, Pauline and Lucy
C F

© The Chicken House 2001

Text © Valerie Mendes 2001
Illustrations © Claire Fletcher 2001

First published in the United Kingdom in 2001 by
The Chicken House, 2 Palmer Street, Frome,
Somerset, BA11 1DS

First paperback publication 2002

Designed by Mandy Sherliker

Printed in U.A.E.

British Library Cataloguing in Publication Data
available. Library of Congress Cataloguing in
Publication data available.

ISBN:1 903434 62 9

Look At Me, Grandma!

Valerie Mendes

Illustrated by Claire Fletcher

The Chicken House

An Egmont joint venture

Just in time, Grandma comes to stay.

"Goodbye, Jamie, darling," says Mum.
"It's time for me to have our baby." She climbs into the car.
"I'll soon be home. Grandma will take you to the park.
And to the beach. And to the Midsummer Fair."
The car speeds away.
"Bye, Mum," Jamie says.

Jamie digs in the sand pit. The sand is burning hot.
At the bottom of the garden the sea lies
calm and blue. Everything is waiting.
Jamie wants to talk to Mum. It's lonely without her.
"Come in for tea," says Grandma.
"You'll soon have a baby to play with."

"Eat up, Jamie," says Grandma.

"I'm not hungry," Jamie says.

The telephone rings. Grandma leaps to answer it.

"Hello?" she says. "Hi, Danny … No news? …
Give her our love. Jamie's fine. Talk to you tomorrow."

"That was Dad," says Grandma. "He sends his love …
I know what we could do.
Let's look at my book of photographs.
I brought it specially to show you."

Grandma opens the book. It is thick and smells of polish.

"There," she says. "That's me when I was your age."

"Who's that?" asks Jamie, pointing.

"That's my big brother, Callum," says Grandma.

"There he is riding his bike …

And there, swimming in the sea.

He had red hair and the brightest green eyes."

"Where is he now?" asks Jamie.

"He died when he was ten. He was ill.

The doctors couldn't save him. It's different today.

Today they would make him well again."

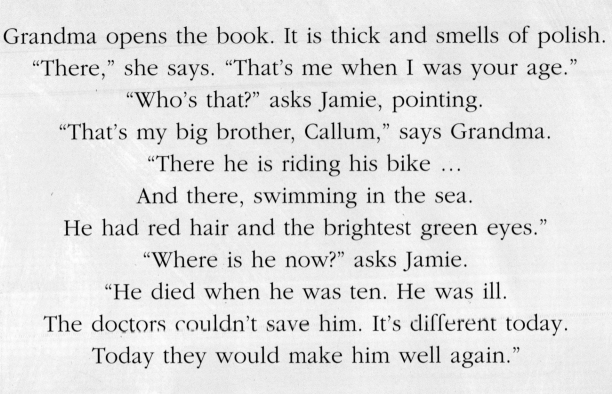

The phone rings again at breakfast.
"Hi, Dad," says Jamie. "How's Mum? …
Oh! … That's wonderful … Lots of love."
"Mum's had our baby," Jamie says.
"Her name's going to be Sara."
"Yes!" says Grandma. She begins to dance.

Jamie runs down to the bottom of the garden.
"I've got a baby sister," he sings to the sea and sky.
"Her name's Sara and she's mine."

That night, Jamie has a dream.
A boy stands by his bed.
He has red hair and the
brightest green eyes.
"My name's Callum,"
he says.
He touches Jamie's
hand. Jamie feels
himself flying.
Out of the window.
Into the garden under
the shining moon.

Callum picks up
Jamie's bicycle.
He begins to pedal
faster than the wind.
"I wish I could do that,"
Jamie says.
"And so you can,"
says Callum.
He pulls Jamie on to
the bike. Then he melts
into the air and Jamie
whirls around and around
the garden on his own.

"Can we go to the park today?"
Jamie asks next morning.
"And can I take my bike?"
On the smooth path, Jamie
grips the handlebars.
Suddenly he isn't
frightened any more.
He begins to pedal.
It feels like moving
faster than the wind.

"Look at me,
Grandma!" he says.

In Jamie's dream that night,
Callum comes again. He
touches Jamie's hand.
Jamie feels himself flying. Out
of the window. Into the garden.
Down to the midnight sea.
Callum begins to swim.
"I wish I could do that,"
Jamie says.
"Here," says Callum.
"Hold on to me."
Then he melts into the waves
and Jamie begins to swim.

"Can we go to the beach
today?" Jamie asks
next morning.
He and Grandma race
down to the sea.
Jamie wades into the waves.
Suddenly he isn't
frightened any more.
He takes the water in his
arms and begins to swim.

"Look at me, Grandma!"
he says.

In Jamie's dream that night,
Callum comes again.
He touches Jamie's hand.
Jamie feels himself flying. Out
of the window. Into the garden.
Across the moonlit sky
to the Midsummer Fair.
Callum strokes a dodgem
car and hums it into life.
They climb aboard. They zoom
it round and round.
Then Callum melts into the
zoom and Jamie drives.

"Can we go to the Midsummer Fair today?"
Jamie asks next morning.
"There's something very special I want to do."
The Fair is hot and crowded.
Jamie pulls Grandma towards the dodgem cars.
He climbs into the driving seat. Grandma sits down
beside him. Jamie hums the engine into life.
And then he drives.

"Look at me, Grandma!" he says.

That night the heatwave breaks.
White sheets of rain sweep from the midnight sky.
Jamie falls deeply asleep.
In his dream he teaches Sara to ride a bike.
To swim in the warm calm sea.
To drive a dodgem car at the Midsummer Fair.

Next morning the doorbell rings. Jamie runs to answer it.
Mum stands on the doorstep, holding a bundle.
"Hello, Jamie, darling," she says. "This is Sara."
She puts the bundle into Jamie's arms.
Jamie looks down at Sara's tiny face.
At her red hair. And the brightest green eyes.

"Look at us, Grandma!" he says.